GEORGE AND MARTHA
ONE FINE DAY

JAMES MARSHALL
HOUGHTON MIFFLIN COMPANY
BOSTON

For my nephew
Alexander Christian Schwartz

Library of Congress Cataloging in Publication Data

Marshall, James, 1942-
  George and Martha, one fine day.

  SUMMARY: Five new episodes in the friendship of the
two hippopotamuses.
  [1. Friendship—Fiction. 2. Hippopotamus—Fiction]
I. Title.
PZ7.M35672Gd   [E]   78-60494
ISBN 0-395-27154-1

Printed in the United States of America

WOZ   30 29 28 27 26

FIVE STORIES

ABOUT

TWO BEST FRIENDS

STORY NUMBER ONE

THE TIGHTROPE

One morning when George looked out his window,

he could scarcely believe his eyes. Martha

was walking a tightrope.

"My stars!" cried George. "I could *never* do that!"

"Why not?" said Martha. "It's tons of fun."

"But it's so high up," said George.

"Yes," said Martha.

"And it's such a long way down," said George.

"That's very true," said Martha.

"It would be quite a fall," said George.

"I see what you mean," said Martha.

Suddenly Martha felt uncomfortable.

For some reason she had lost all her confidence.

She began to wobble.

George realized his mistake.

Now he had to do some fast talking.

"Of course," he said, "anyone can see you love walking the tightrope."

"Oh, yes?" said Martha.

"Certainly," said George. "And if you love what you do, you'll be very good at it too."

Martha's confidence was restored.

"Watch this!" she said. Martha did some fancy footwork on her tightrope.

STORY NUMBER TWO

THE DIARY

Whenever Martha sat down to write in her
diary, George was always nearby.

"Yes, George?" said Martha.

"I was just on my way to the kitchen," said George.

"Hum," said Martha.

Martha decided to finish writing outdoors.
"How peculiar," she said to herself. "I can
still smell George's cologne."
Then Martha heard leaves rustling above her.

"Aha!" she cried. "You were spying on me!"

"I wanted to see what you were writing in your diary," said George.

"Then you should have asked my permission," said Martha.

"May I peek in your diary?" asked George politely.

"No," said Martha.

STORY NUMBER

THREE

THE ICKY STORY

At lunch George started to tell an icky story.

Martha strongly objected.

"Please, have some consideration," she said.

But George told his icky story nevertheless.

"You're asking for it," said Martha.

When Martha finished her lunch, *she* told
an icky story. It was so icky that George
felt all queasy inside. He couldn't even
eat his dessert.

"You're the champ," said George.

"Don't make me do it again," said Martha.

"I won't," said George.

"Boo!" cried George.

"Have mercy!" screamed Martha.

Martha and her stamp collection went flying.

"I'm sorry," said George. "I was feeling wicked."

"Well," said Martha. "Now it's my turn."

"Go ahead," said George.

"Not right away," said Martha slyly.

Suddenly George found it very difficult to concentrate on what he was doing.

"Any minute now, Martha is going to scare the pants off me," he said to himself.

"Maybe she is hiding someplace," he said.
George made sure that Martha wasn't hiding
under the sink.

During the day George
got more and more nervous.
"Any minute now," he said.

But Martha was relaxing in her hammock.

"I'm sorry I forgot to scare you," said Martha.

"That's all right," said George. "It wouldn't have worked anyway. I'm not easily frightened."

"I know," said Martha.

THE LAST STORY

STORY

TICKETS

THE AMUSEMENT PARK

That evening George and Martha
went to the amusement park.
They rode the ferris wheel.

They rode the roller coaster.

They rode the bump cars.

They were having a wonderful time.

But in the Tunnel of Love, Martha
sat very quiet.
It was very very dark in there.
Suddenly Martha cried "Boo!"
"Have mercy!" screamed George.
"I didn't forget after all," said Martha.
"So I see," said George.